For Coyot

who sees the magic beneath the waves

Viking

Published by the Penguin Group, Penguin Group (USA) LLC

375 Hudson Street, New York, New York 10014

USA ✱ Canada ✱ UK ✱ Ireland ✱ Australia ✱ New Zealand ✱ India ✱ South Africa ✱ China

penguin.com

A Penguin Random House Company

First published in the United States of America by Viking, an imprint of Penguin Young Readers Group, 2014

LIBRARY OF CONGRESS CATALOGING-IN-PUBLICATION DATA

Marino, Gianna, author, illustrator.

Following Papa's song / by Gianna Marino.

pages cm

Summary: "Little Blue, a young humpback whale, has never made the long migration up the coast, and he is worried about his first long journey with Papa"—Provided by publisher.

ISBN 978-0-670-01315-9 (hardback)

[1. Humpback whale—Fiction. 2. Whales—Fiction. 3. Animals—Migration—Fiction. 4. Father and child—Fiction.] I. Title.

PZ7.M33882Fo 2014   [E]—dc23   2013024213

10 9 8 7 6 5 4 3 2 1

Manufactured in China   Book design by Nancy Brennan   Set in Archer

These mixed media illustrations were created with gouache and gum arabic on Saunders Waterford Watercolour Paper and mulberry paper.

Following Papa's
SONG

by

Gianna Marino

Viking
An Imprint of Penguin Group (USA)

AT DAWN, Little Blue nuzzled alongside Papa and asked, "Is it time?"
"Listen for the other whales," said Papa. "When you hear their call,
we'll know it's time to go."

Little Blue listened to the peaceful quiet that whispered through the morning sea.

"Papa?" asked Little Blue.

"Are we going very far?"

"Yes, Little Blue. We will travel farther than we have ever gone before."

"But Papa? How will we know which way to go?"

"We'll follow the song of the whales, Little Blue,
just like our family has for years upon years."

Papa moved off with a sweep of his tail, and Little Blue wiggled to follow.

"Papa!" said Little Blue. "How do you swim so fast!?"

"When you are big, Little Blue,
your tail will carry you quickly, too."

"When I am big, Papa,
will I still hear your song?"

"Yes, Little Blue.
If you listen closely,
you will always hear
my song."

Little Blue heard a sound from far off and said,
"I hear the other whales, Papa! I hear them!"

"Yes, Little Blue. Now it's time to begin our journey."
Papa's voice echoed across the sea, through the liquid
light and deep into the mysterious black.

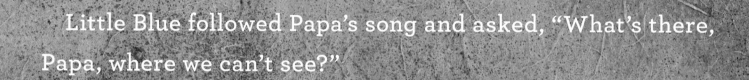

Little Blue followed Papa's song and asked, "What's there,
Papa, where we can't see?"

"Ahead is our summer feeding ground, Little Blue. And below
us is a magical world," said Papa. "But far below, it is very dark."

As they traveled, Little Blue dreamed of what lay below
and saw a flash in the darkness.

With a *swoosh* of a tail, Little Blue followed the flickering light and dove down, into the cool water.

Everything *was* magical, just
like Papa said.

Little Blue went deeper . . .

. . . far below.

It was cold

and dark

and silent.

"PAPA! WHERE ARE YOU?" cried Little Blue.

"WHERE ARE YOUUUUUUUU

UUUUUUUUUUUUUUUUUUU

But Little Blue's small voice was lost in the darkness.

Then Little Blue remembered what Papa said . . .

and listened.

Little Blue followed the path of Papa's song and rose up from the deep.

Together they soared into the light . . .

. . . and sang Papa's song across the evening sea.